Noisy Farm

Rod Campbell

MACMILLAN CHILDREN'S BOOKS

It's daybreak on the farm.
'Cockadoodle-doo!' says
the rooster.
'Wake up, wake up!'

'Woof, woof!'
Sam the farm dog is awake.
He can hear lots of
different noises.

Sam can hear a chugging noise.
What can that be?

It's the tractor
off to plough the fields.

Where's Sam?

Sam can hear a running noise.
What can that be?

It's the rabbit
running home.

Where are her babies?

Sam can hear a mooing noise.
What can that be?

It's the cow
in the barn.

Where is her calf?

Sam can hear an oinking noise.
What can that be?

It's the pig
in the pigsty.

Where are her piglets?

Sam can hear a clucking noise.
What can that be?

It's the hen
in the hen house.

Where are her chicks?

Sam can hear a baaing noise.
What can that be?

It's the sheep
in the field.

Where is her lamb?

Sam can hear a quacking noise.
What can that be?

But listen . . .
There's a loud snoring noise
coming from the barn!

Who can that be?

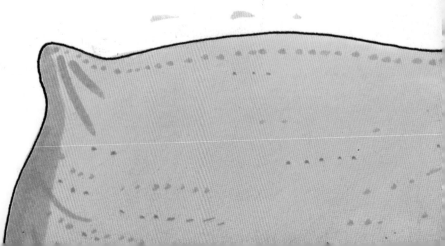

Shh! Let's leave him to sleep!

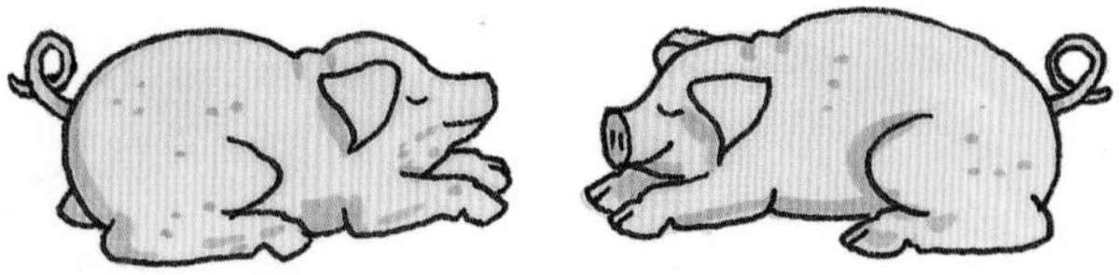